Max & Milo
Go to Sleep!
by Heather & Ethan Long
Aladdin · New York London Toronto Sydney New Delhi

To Cooper and Carson,
our real-life Max and Milo
—H.L. and E.L.

ALADDIN • An imprint of Simon & Schuster Children's Publishing Division • 1230 Avenue of the Americas, New York, NY 10020 • First Aladdin hardcover edition January 2013 • • For information about special discounts for bulk purchases, please contact Simon & Schuster Special Sales at 1-866-506-1949 or business@simonandschuster.com. •

The Simon & Schuster Speakers Bureau can bring authors to your live event. For more information or to book an event contact the Simon & Schuster Speakers Bureau at 1-866-248-3049 or visit our website at www.simonspeakers.com. • Designed by Lisa Vega • The text of this book was set in Chaloops Medium and ChaloopsDecaf. • The illustrations for this book were rendered digitally. • Manufactured in China 1012 SCP • 10 9 8 7 6 5 4 3 2 1 • This book is cataloged with the Library of Congress • ISBN 978-1-4424-5143-8 • ISBN 978-1-4424-5144-5 (eBook)

Good night, Max.

Good night, Milo.
The Legend of Sleepy Hollow

MAX! Wake up!
I can't sleep.

You've only been trying for two seconds. Why don't you read a book?
Good idea!

Read that one . . .
Too scary . . .
Too long . . .
Too short . . .
Too sad . . .

Aha!
My favorite.
The Adventures of BUCK FINN

click
BUCK FINN

click
click
click
BUCK FINN

click
click
click
click
click
click
MAX! Wake up!
My lamp is broken.
Then get a
flashlight.
That is a
good idea. . . .

HA! HA! HA! HA! HA! HA! This is the funniest book EVER!
The Legend of Sleepy Hollow

MAX!
Wake up!
This light
is making me
hot.

Then find the fan.
Good idea!

Perfect spot.
CLICK

WHIRRRRRRR
Boy, this fan is making my throat dry!

MAX! Wake up!
Now I'm thirsty.

Then get a glass of water.
Good idea!

SLUR
The Adventures of BUCK FINN

RRRP!
Legend of Sleepy Hollow

Mmm. NOW
I can sleep.
Good night,
Max.

Good night,
Milo.

MAX! I still can't sleep.

Well, maybe you should just be STILL for once!
The Legend of Sleepy Hollow

You do this EVERY NIGHT!
You never really try to go to sleep.
You can never find your books.
YAWN

You're ALWAYS thirsty.
Do you need to build a silly contraption for EVERYTHING?!?
And, Milo, take those goofy pajamas off your head!!!

FUTBOL
Milo?
The Legend of Sleepy Hollow

Whew! At last, I can go to bed.
Sleepy Hollow

** s i g h **
How will I ever get to sleep?
The Legend of Sleepy Hollow

Good idea, Milo.
Good idea.
The Adventures of BUCK FINN
The Legend of Sleepy Hollow